Dear Frank

Also by W. Nikola-Lisa:

BOOKS FOR YOUNG READERS
America: A Book of Opposites
Bein' With You This Way
Can You Top That?
My Teacher Can Teach... *Anyone!*
Night Is Coming
One Hole in the Road
Setting the Turkeys Free
Shake Dem Halloween Bones
Summer Sun Risin'
Tangletalk

BOOKS FOR OLDER READERS
Dragonfly: A Childhood Memoir
How We Are Smart
Magic in the Margins
The Year With Grandma Moses
Till Year's Good End

BOOKS FOR PARENTS AND TEACHERS
Hey, Aren't You the Janitor? And Other Tales
from the Life of a Children's Book Author

Dear Frank

BABE RUTH, THE RED SOX, AND THE GREAT WAR

W. Nikola-Lisa

With illustrations by Hugh Spector

Gyroscope Books

Chicago

Copyright © 2011 by W. Nikola-Lisa

All rights reserved.
No part of this book may be reproduced or transmitted in any form
or by any means, electronic or mechanical, including photocopying,
recording, or by any information storage and retrieval system, without
the written permission of the publisher, except where permitted by law.

Library of Congress Information
Author: Nikola-Lisa, W. [American, b.1951]
Summary: A set of letters from one brother to another captures the
mood of a family during World War I and the events leading up to the
1918 World Series.

With special thanks to Tom Greensfelder for cover design and layout.

Cover Photo Credits: Top photo from Wikimedia Commons. 1918
Boston Red Sox. Babe Ruth last row, arms crossed, fourth from left.
Source: Heritage Auction Gallery. Author: Carl Horner. Date of photo:
1918. Bottom photo from the collection of Vincent Petty. 2nd Battalion,
318th Infantry Regiment baseball team aboard the USS Maui. Source:
www.hardscrabblefarm.com. Proprietor: Brian Mead. Date of photo:
1919.

ISBN-13: 978-0-9912183-6-3
ISBN-10: 0991218361
LCCN: 2011963374

Gyroscope Books
Chicago

To Dylan

Born to play the game.
Lives to play the game.

*Baseball was, is and always will be
to me the best game in the world.*
–Babe Ruth

I've long been interested in the history of major league baseball. While reading about baseball in the Boston area during the first two decades of the 20th century, I became interested in the war-shortened 1918 season.

As World War I raged on the battlefields of Europe, major league baseball fought its own war at home with U.S. War Secretary Newton Baker, who had declared professional baseball "non-productive work." His decision meant that players had to find productive work or face being drafted into the army.

Frightened by the work-or-fight order, many players left their team to work in factories or shipyards. Baseball owners, however, pleaded with the War Secretary to let the season finish. After weeks of talks and indecision, the War

Secretary finally declared that the regular season would end after Labor Day weekend, and be followed by a best-out-of-seven-games World Series.

The two teams that squared off against each other were the Chicago Cubs and the Boston Red Sox. By 1918, the Red Sox were the hottest team in baseball, having won several World Series Championship titles. They did so with one of the best players in the game — George Herman "Babe" Ruth. Ruth not only distinguished himself as one of professional baseball's best left-handed pitchers, but also as one of its best hitters.

By the spring of 1918, if you lived in the Boston area, there was little else to talk about but Babe Ruth, the Red Sox, and the Great War. –*W.N.-L.*

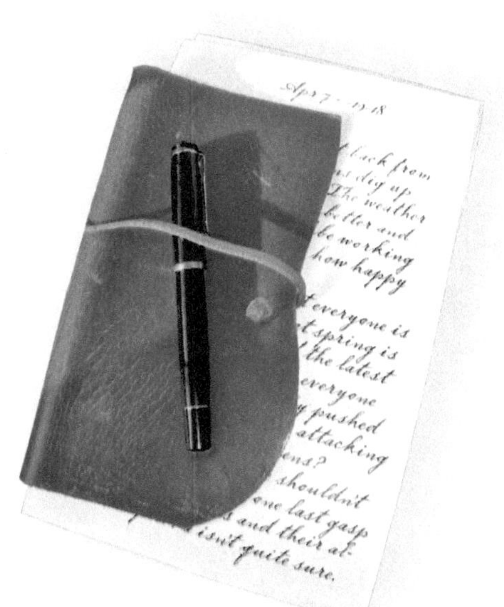
Apr 7 - 1918
back from
dig up
The weather
better and
be working
how happy
everyone is
spring is
the latest
everyone
pushed
attacking
ens?
shouldn't
one last gasp
and their at-
isn't quite sure.

<u>March 20, 1918</u>

Dear Frank,

    I bet you're surprised to get a letter from me. Mom said I should write to you on my own, that you'd enjoy getting a letter from your younger brother. She's right of course. And since she's been so good at writing to you, I guess I should do the same. Anyway, at least I could keep you up on the latest news while you're overseas.

It's been pretty quiet around here this past month. Pa's been working hard at Mr. Decker's factory making truck parts for the army. Mom's working long hours at the hospital since they're short on staff.

I've been trying to do my part, too. I've already asked the Thrashers and the Paulsens if I could help them with their victory garden once the weather turns nice. Mom says everyone has to pitch in now that America has entered the war.

Uncle Roger has stopped by a lot lately. He brings us the latest news about the war. He says it will be over soon, probably by summer, especially now that General Pershing is in France commanding the American troops.

I don't know what we'd do without Uncle Roger. He's always so cheery. It's good for us, especially Mom, who misses you so much.

By the way, Uncle Roger thinks the Red Sox will win the pennant this year. If they do it will be their third pennant in four years. We all hope you're well.

Your brother,
Andrew

<u>April 7, 1918</u>

Dear Frank,

I just got back from helping the Paulsens dig up their garden beds. The weather has turned for the better and soon everyone will be working outside. You know how happy that makes Mom.

I'd like to say that everyone is happy here, now that spring is upon us, but news of the latest German offensive has everyone worried. Is it true they pushed into French territory, attacking the British near Amiens?

Uncle Roger says we shouldn't worry, that it's just one last gasp before the Germans and their allies collapse. Pa isn't quite sure. He says that President Wilson should send more American troops to help the French and

British, especially now that the Russians are out of the war.

That's how it goes every night, Uncle Roger and Pa arguing about the war, and Mom sitting quietly, listening, but not saying a word. I know in the back of her mind she's only thinking about you.

She doesn't care if more Americans join the war or not. She doesn't care about President Wilson, or the

Russians. She only cares about you, and wants you home safe and sound.

When Uncle Roger and Pa aren't talking about the war, they're talking baseball. A lot of people think there shouldn't be a season this year, what with the war and all.

I guess a lot of players feel the same way since over a hundred players in both leagues failed to show up for spring training.

Pa says that's good. Men their age should enlist, or at least work in a factory or a shipyard.

Uncle Roger disagrees. He thinks playing baseball is as important as joining the service. Well, at least as important as working in a factory.

I think he's right, too. I don't know what people in Boston would do if they didn't have the Red Sox to talk about.

Speaking of the Red
Sox, they won their first
exhibition game the other
day against Brooklyn. And
guess where Ruth played?
In the outfield! And he
belted two home runs. Uncle
Roger says that's a very good
sign. I think so, too.
　　Take care, Frank.

　　　　Write soon,
　　　　Andrew

<u>April 16, 1918</u>

Dear Frank,

    We got your last letter. You don't know how much it means to Mom to get a letter from you. She keeps all of your letters in a small box on her bureau. Sometimes when I get home from school I'll find her sitting in the kitchen by the window, box in lap, pouring over your letters.

Between your letters and news of the war, I can't keep all of the names and places straight. Pa tries to help me, but it's even hard for him.

Uncle Roger bought me an atlas to help. I keep it on my nightstand next to my bed. Every night I look at it and try to imagine where you are and what your company's doing.

We were all relieved to hear that the latest German

offensive near Ypres, on the French-Belgian border, has stalled, and that Allied forces are now under one command.

Of course, Uncle Roger and Pa disagree on this. Pa thinks it's a good idea that Allied forces are under the command of Marshal Foch, the senior French general.

Uncle Roger takes the opposite view. He thinks that the Americans should be under their own command, whether it's Pershing or some other general.

Right now it seems you can't escape all the talk about the war. Last week, when Uncle Roger was in New York City on business, he went to a war rally in Times Square.

Thousands of people came out to hear several celebrities speak in support of the war. Charlie Chaplin and Mary Pickford were among them. It seems the whole country is caught up in war fever.

But you're probably more interested in hearing about baseball.

You'll be pleased to know that the Red Sox won on Opening Day. According to the newspapers, it was a grand affair. Everyone was cheering, including the Royal Rooters, who were out in full force, yelling at the top of their lungs when last year's pennant was hoisted.

After the Red Sox did a close-drill march using

their bats as rifles, Ruth
came out and pitched a great
game, beating Philadelphia
7-1. It's his third Opening
Day win in a row. Wow, he
sure can pitch! That's it,
Frank.

We miss you,
Andrew

Dear Frank,

Sorry I haven't written lately, but I've been thinking about you. We all have. And there's lots of news to catch you up on.

First of all, you would be surprised to know that the Patriot's Day marathon was canceled, and in its place the Boston Athletic Association sponsored a servicemen's relay race. Servicemen from Camp Devens, the Boston Navy Yard, the Naval Cadet School, and the Signal Battalion participated, each fielding a team of ten men.

They ran a marathon, but each member of the team only ran two-and-a half miles. Uncle Roger said that's because they didn't have time to train properly to run a full marathon.

You'll be happy to know,

since you did basic training there, that the team
from Camp Devens won
handily. They looked so
smart in their khaki suits
and leggings, as did the
Navy Yard boys in their
bright white suits.

Pa was less optimistic.
He said the entire event was
one big promotional gim-
mick for the war. In each
baton that the men carried
there was a message that
read:

We will fight to the limit;
we expect you to buy
war bonds to the limit.

Pa says that sometimes
the Liberty Loan Commit-
tee goes a little too far in
promoting the war. Every-
where you look there's an ad
encouraging people to buy
war bonds.

Uncle Roger says
that buying war bonds is
important. The more bonds
people buy, the more supplies

the government can send to
our troops.

Anyway, I've been try-
ing to do my part. With the
extra money I make doing
chores, I've been buying war
stamps. I've almost filled up
an entire book.

When it's filled, Uncle
Roger said he would take me
to the bank to trade it in for
a war bond. It's not a bad
deal. To fill a book with
stamps will cost $18.75, but
when I cash the bond in it

will be worth a whopping $25.

Hey, Frank, how about those Red Sox? They're off to their best start ever. They went unbeaten in their first six games. Now they're 12-3. And Ruth's been hitting almost .500 this month, with three home runs.

I'm keeping a scrapbook of the Red Sox's season, since I figure you'll want to know everything that happens when you return. Uncle Roger said it's a great idea. So did

Pa. Even Mom smiled when
I told her what I was doing.
What do you think, Frank,
a good idea?

Yours as always,
Andrew

<u>May 31, 1918</u>

Dear Frank,

Yesterday was Decoration Day. Well, I guess I should say Memorial Day since there's talk of changing the name. Instead of remembering soldiers who died in the Civil War, which is what Decoration Day commemorated, on Memorial Day we'll remember American soldiers who died in any war.

You should have seen the festivities. Flag bunting streamed from every railing and lamppost in town. At noon there was a parade down Main Street. Everybody turned out to see it, cheering and waving American flags. The mayor spoke. So did someone from the Liberty Loan Committee who read President Wilson's Memorial Day message.

All was so cheery and festive until a company of

wounded soldiers turned
the corner and marched down
Main Street. Mothers qui-
eted their children. Men
stood at attention. It was
an eerie reminder that the
war, as far away as it seems,
has touched a lot of people.

Afterwards we had a
picnic with the Murphy
and Gorman families.
Everyone asked about you,
Frank. I told them you were
fine, though we haven't had
a letter from you lately. It

really upsets Mom when she doesn't get a letter from you.

Sometimes I'll find her sitting alone, crying. I know she's thinking about you. I give her a hug and tell her you'll be all right, and not to worry. She just smiles and squeezes my arm. She really misses you, Frank.

We went over to Uncle Roger's for dinner the other night. After talk about the latest German offensive, Uncle Roger and Pa talked

baseball the whole night.
I guess there's a lot to talk
about.

Several weeks ago the
person in charge of the draft,
General Crowder, ruled that
baseball was not an essential
activity. That means that
players are supposed to join
the army or find work in a
war-related industry.

Wow, did that make
Uncle Roger hot under the
collar. He said that if actors
don't have to enlist, why do

baseball players? Aren't actors and baseball players both entertainers?

Some of the team owners have petitioned Secretary Baker, the War Secretary, to postpone General Crowder's order. It doesn't look good right now though. Write soon. We all look forward to hearing from you.

Your brother,
Andrew

June 15, 1918

Dear Frank,

We've been following closely the latest German offensive near Soissons and Château-Thierry. Are they really shelling Paris?

Pa says your unit is in the area. But Uncle Roger says not to worry, if anyone can stop the Germans our doughboys can.

When I asked Pa why

American soldiers are called doughboys, he said it's because they're always covered with dirt from fighting in the trenches all day. Uncle Roger laughed and said it's really because people from Europe think American soldiers are young and rich.

I guess doughboys is better than what members of your unit are called back home—nutmeggers—and just because you're all from New

England. Of course it could be worse, Frank, you could be called maple-syrupers.

Speaking of names, Uncle Roger has been calling Secretary Baker lots of names lately. The Secretary still hasn't decided whether or not major league baseball should be considered pro-ductive work. If it's not, then the season will fold as players leave to join the army or find war-related work.

It's left Uncle Roger

kind of grumpy lately,
mainly because the Red
Sox are in first place, and
it's all because of this fellow
Ruth the Red Sox picked up
a couple of years ago. He's a
terror on the mound—and at
the plate! It really would be
a shame if the season were cut
short.

You can read all about
it when you return. Uncle
Roger's been bringing me the
newspaper every couple of
days so I can clip stories

about the Red Sox for my
scrapbook. You should see it,
Frank, and it's only the
middle of June. I can't wait
to show you—really!

Take care,
Andrew

July 10, 1918

Dear Frank,

I can't tell you how relieved Mom was to get your last letter, what with you in the midst of all the fighting. It seems like every time we pick up the papers all there is are stories about the latest German offensive.

Last week, at the 4th of July celebration, that's all anybody talked about. We had a picnic in the park and then watched the fireworks later. My favorite ones are the large starbursts. Mom likes those, too.

Gracie, your old girlfriend, stopped by to ask about you. She sure looks pretty in a summer dress, Frank. I told her you were fine. She smiled and told me to tell you that she's been thinking about you and hopes you'll be home soon.

Mom looked great, too.

I think it's the first time I've seen her relax in a long time. I can't tell you how much she misses you.

Of course, Uncle Roger was there, talking baseball. Everyone was, now that Secretary Baker finally made a decision.

Two weeks ago he announced that baseball was not essential work, which means that players will have to find war-related work or join the army. Uncle Roger was fuming, even though General Crowder said he wouldn't enforce the ruling right away.

Secretary Baker's decision also scared a lot of players, including Ruth who left the Red Sox at the beginning of July to work at the Chester Shipyards in Pennsylvania. Man, did that create a stir in the papers. Pa said not to pay it any attention. It's all a big bluff.

Well, it turns out Pa was

right. Ruth was back in the Red Sox lineup for a 4th of July doubleheader in Philadelphia against the Athletics. Since then, the Red Sox have been cleaning up.

They just beat the Indians four out of five games. And all because of this guy Ruth. He sure can swing a bat, Frank. He hit his eleventh home run on June 30, and now leads the league in homers. Not bad for a pitcher!

Get home soon, Frank.
We all miss you. Mom the
most.

Yours,
Andrew

July 3-1, -19-18

Dear Frank,

    Things have really been happening since the last time I wrote to you. Remember how I told you Secretary Baker announced that major league baseball was not an essential war occupation. Well, as soon as he made the announcement the president of the American League declared that the American

League season would end on July 2-1.

But hardly any of the owners agreed with him, including the owner of the Red Sox. He and several other owners opposed to ending the season early went directly to Secretary Baker and pleaded with him to let the season finish at the end of September.

After several meetings, and lots of articles in the newspapers, Secretary Baker finally made a ruling: the regular baseball season will end after the Labor Day weekend. Only he didn't say whether there would be a World Series after that.

Uncle Roger was beside himself. He kept ranting and raving, "When will he decide? When will he decide?" He ranted and raved until Mom pulled a cherry pie out of the oven. That settled him down pretty quickly.

As soon as Secretary Baker makes a decision on the World Series I'll let you know. Meanwhile, the Red Sox are still tearing up the league and should clinch first place any day.

By the way, we were all saddened to hear of the downing of Quentin Roosevelt over German lines. The former President's youngest son loved to fly, and he was so full of American spirit. Just like his father.

Can't wait to see you,
Frank.

I mean it,
Andrew

August 14, 1918

Dear Frank,

We got your last letter, or I should say letters since we got two of them on the same day. I guess one of them got lost in the military mail for a while.

Mom's been worried sick about you. When your letters arrived she was beside herself with joy. Pa perked up, too.

Other families aren't so lucky though.

Last week the McCrackens down the road got word that their son, Thomas, was killed at Amiens as the Allies beat back another German attack.

You remember Thomas. He was a year ahead of you in school. We haven't seen Mrs. McCracken now for the better part of a week. Mom goes over every other day or so to sit with her.

Lately, the papers have been filled with a growing list of war casualties. I think that's why Mom doesn't read the newspapers anymore. The headlines are always the same: "Gassed Dorchester Soldier's Funeral Today." "Boston Flyer Downed." "Lowell Guardsman Killed In Action." I think Mom's afraid that one day she'll be reading about you.

There was news to lift everyone's spirits this week however. It appears that the last German offensive has failed. Even the German High Command called it a "Black Day for the German Army."

Uncle Roger said it was all because of how the American forces fought. They must have fought bravely because the French President awarded the Grand Cross of the Legion of Honor to General Pershing for successfully leading the American counterattack.

Now Uncle Roger's convinced the war will be over by the end of the month. And that means there will be a World Series. If there is, Uncle Roger said he would take us to one of the games. That is, if the Red Sox win the pennant.

Imagine that, Frank, you and me at a World Series game rooting for the Red Sox. Now that's something to come home to. Right?

By the way, Frank,

is there any word on when
you'll be home? We're all
waiting to hear from you on
that. Let us know as soon
as you find out.

Your brother,
Andrew

August 28, 1918

Dear Frank,

My head is swimming. There is so much to tell you since the last time I wrote. First of all, Secretary Baker finally made a decision: there will be a World Series this year, and it will start on Thursday, September 5.

The Chicago Cubs won the National League pennant by ten-and-a-half games.

And guess who won the American League pennant?

That's right, Frank, the Red Sox! They clinched the pennant today when they beat Philadelphia 6–1 with Ruth on the mound. So, it's the Cubs against the Red Sox.

Uncle Roger hates the Cubs. He still remembers the 1907 and 1908 World Series when the National Leaguers whupped the American League Tigers. But that didn't stop him from hopping on the first train to Boston to pick up tickets to one of the games.

Yes, Frank, we're going to a World Series game. The first three games will be played in Chicago. Then the teams will head to Boston to play the final games. Let's hope for a long series.

Pa's as excited as Uncle Roger. Mom's quiet on the matter. I don't think it's because she doesn't like baseball. I think it's because Uncle Roger insists on buying a ticket for you whether you're here or not.

The thought of watching a World Series game in Boston next to an empty seat reserved for you makes Mom really sad. I don't think it'll hit Uncle Roger or Pa until they actually see that empty seat next to them.

Frank, you've got to get home by Sunday, September 8. That's the day the teams arrive in Boston.

Uncle Roger is going to get us tickets for Tuesday's game at Fenway.

Frank, you've got to make it home by then! Everyone's counting on it.

Please hurry,
Andrew

September 8, 1918

Dear Frank,

It's Sunday night. Uncle Roger's been over the last couple of days jawing about the World Series with Pa.

The Red Sox won the first game on Thursday with Ruth on the mound. He didn't do much at the plate, but he pitched a whale of a game. The Red Sox won 1-0.

The next day the Cubs

beat the Red Sox in another close game. Ruth didn't play since he had pitched the day before. The Red Sox came back on Saturday, squeaking by the Cubs 2–1 to take two out of three games in Chicago.

Now they head east to finish the series in Boston.

We're still hopeful you'll make it home. Mom said she wouldn't go if you weren't here. Uncle Roger said, "Don't be silly, of course you'll go.

Frankie would want you to!"

Pa didn't say anything for a long time, and then he mentioned that perhaps none of us should go.

Everyone looked at him in disbelief. Then he explained that it might not be safe, what with the flu epidemic at Camp Devens spreading to Boston.

Uncle Roger reminded him that just last week there was a big war rally at Fenway Park, and that thousands of people showed up for it.

Well, whether we go or not, it just won't be the same if you don't make it home in time for the game. Sometimes I imagine that you'll walk in the door just as we're getting ready to leave.

Can't you ask your sergeant or some general if you could be excused from the war? It would make everyone really happy if you made it home.

If you don't I promise
to make a full account of the
game in my scrapbook. You
should see it. It's really
filling up. You'll be able to
read about the whole season
when you return.

You will return, Frank,
won't you?

Your brother,
Andrew

Dear Frank,

It should be a day of joy. Yesterday the Red Sox won the World Series, and the day before that we went to the fifth game of the Series, the first time I've ever seen a professional baseball game.

Everyone went, even Mom. But it was strange. There we were, the four of us—Uncle Roger, Pa, Mom, and me—with five tickets.

Pa wanted to invite one of the guys from the factory, but Mom said no, we would hold the seat empty for you.

And we did, Frank.

But seeing the empty seat, Uncle Roger and Pa just sat there, sad-faced. When the game started, and we stood to sing "The Star-Spangled Banner," we could hardly utter a word we were so choked up.

Mom, who probably

misses you the most, sur-
prised us though.

After we sat down, and
the game got underway,
Mom opened her handbag
and pulled out your glove
and set it on the empty seat.

Pa looked at her for a
moment, then leaned over
and gave her a big kiss.

After that we started
rooting as hard as we could
for the Red Sox. And even
though they lost, and Ruth
didn't play because of a banged

up finger, it was the best baseball game I've ever seen.

After the game, we walked to the train station and headed home. When we got there, Mom made a great dinner. Afterwards, Pa and Uncle Roger played cards late into the night, talking about the game the whole time.

This morning Uncle Roger took me downtown to get the first paper off the newsstand to read about the Red Sox.

They won, Frank! They beat the Cubs.

They're champs.

It's their third World Series title in four years. And do you know who the key player was for the Red Sox?

No, it wasn't Ruth.

It was George Whiteman who took Ruth's place in the outfield. Whiteman made several key plays and had the best batting average in the series. Ruth got into

the last game, but only in
the seventh inning after
Whiteman hurt himself.

That's it, Frank. The
season is over, the Red Sox
are World Series champs, and
you're still not home. Uncle
Roger says not to worry; the
war will be over soon.

This time I think he
might be right. The 1st
army division just launched
a massive attack against the
Germans at St Mihiel. If
they win there, and in the

Argonne forest near Meuse,
the war will all but be over.
Let's hope so, Frank. We miss
you. It's just not the same
around here without you.

See you soon,
Andrew

<u>October 14, 1918</u>

Dear Frank,

    It's been a month since I last wrote you. We all keep waiting for news of an armistice. The Germans have been retreating for almost six weeks. Uncle Roger says, in his usual cheery voice, "Any day now!" This time Pa agrees with him: the war will be over any day now.

    Mom's been quiet on the

matter, until wounded soldiers returning from Europe
said the same thing. And
you know what that means,
Frank? You'll be coming
home! You don't know how
happy that makes all of us
here. Mom is beside herself.
All she talks about is
making your favorite din-
ners for you.

Pa's happy, too. He says
that when the war is finally
over, and he can take a little
time off from work, he's going

to take both of us on a long fishing trip next spring. Although he doesn't talk about it much, I know your being away has been hard on him, too.

Uncle Roger is also happy. He can't wait to see you. He said he'd buy tickets to as many Red Sox games as you like, enough tickets for all of us.

I'm happy, Frank. I can't wait to have my big brother home again. And

I have a surprise for you.
I finished the scrapbook.
It's chock full of articles,
photographs, and programs—
anything I could lay my
hands on. I even have your
unused ticket to the fifth
game of the 1918 World Series
in it as well. I thought you
might like that.

Well, I guess that's it.
Before you know it, you'll be
home and we'll be a family
again. I can't wait to see
my big brother. I've really

missed you, Frank. We all
have.

> Yours as always,
> Andrew

P.S. Uncle Roger was right. Despite his poor batting average during the World Series, Ruth is moving to the outfield full time next season. Not only that, but Mom said she wants to go to the games with us. Imagine that, Mom, a Red Sox fan. Next thing you know she'll want her own glove.

*And what about Frank?
Did he return from the war?*

Chances are he did, but not immediately. After Germany signed an armistice with Western Allies on Nov. 11, 1918, it took over a year for the U.S. to withdraw its troops. Doing so earlier would have left a power vacuum in the territories of the defeated Central European Allies.

The loss of life as a result of the war was staggering: an estimated 8 million military casualties alone. Of those, 117,000 were U.S. soldiers, or less than 2% of total military losses.

So, chances are Frank returned home — a little older, a little wiser, and extremely grateful to be reunited with his family.

IN THE CLASSROOM

I wrote *Dear Frank* using an epistolary or letter format. I'm not the first to use this approach. Ring Lardner, the great American humorist and sports columnist, used this format almost a century ago in his novel *You Know Me Al*, a satirical look at the baseball world of his day written as a series of letters by his protagonist Jack Keefe, a bush-league player, to a hometown friend. Writers of youth literature are no strangers to this format as well. Here are a few of my favorite authors and the stories they've written using an epistolary or letter format.

FOR YOUNG READERS

I remember opening Janet and Allan Ahlberg's *The Jolly Postman* (LB Kids, 2001, originally published in 1987) and thinking that this was a very inventive book for young readers. Not only is it written in letter format, but the letters are tucked inside actual envelopes. The recipients of the letters are familiar fairy tale characters, delivered by a most jolly postman.

Alma Flor Ada uses a similar format in her book *Dear Peter Rabbit* (Atheneum, 1997), the first of several epistolary books by Ada for young readers. In this collection of letters by fairy tale characters, reminiscent of the Ahlberg's *Jolly Postman*, Ada weaves together a story of mystery and intrigue, all through a series of crisscrossing letters.

Judith Caseley, in *Dear Annie* (Green-willow, 1994), relates the tender rela-tionship between Annie and her grandpa in a series of letters that begins at Annie's birth (answered by her mother at first) and continues into her childhood (when Annie can write her own letters). Proud of her new pen pal, Annie takes her box of letters to school for show-and-tell.

Mark Teague's *Dear Mrs. LaRue: Letters from Obedience School* (Scholastic, 2002) is a hilarious send-up of canine life as seen from the perspective of Ike, an unrepentant pooch "sentenced" to obedience school. Through a series of guilt-inducing letters, Ike tries to per-suade his owner, Mrs. LaRue, to spring him from Brotweiler Canine Academy, the apparent source of his misery.

FOR OLDER READERS

In 1983, Beverly Cleary published her groundbreaking work, *Dear Mr. Henshaw* (Scholastic, 1983), the Newberry award-winning story of Leigh Botts who, through a series of letters and journal writing, establishes a warm relationship with his favorite author, Mr. Henshaw. Although Mr. Henshaw takes his time to respond to Leigh's letters, when he does he encourages Leigh to keep a journal, which the young scrivener does, further inspiring his writing interests.

An equally engaging novel is Steve Kluger's *Last Days of Summer* (Morrow, 2008, originally published in 1998), in which a young Jewish boy, twelve-year-old Joey Margolis, corresponds with his favorite baseball player, the fictional New York Giants third baseman Charlie Banks. Unlike Cleary's characters, Kluger's interact often, sharing the ups and downs of their different worlds. Kluger also doesn't restrict himself exclusively to letters, but also interjects postcards, interviews, progress reports, and newspaper clippings.

Finally, for the older reader, I suggest Stephen Ohbosky's debut novel, *The Perks of Being a Wallflower* (MTV Books, 1999). Charlie, a high school freshman, reveals his world through a series of letters written to someone of undisclosed name, age, and gender. It's a stylistic gem, appropriate for the mature reader who learns of Charlie's many struggles as he teeters on the brink of adulthood.

W. Nikola-Lisa is an accomplished
storyteller and award-winning author.
www.nikolabooks.com

Hugh Spector is a visual artist who
specializes in collage and story boxes.
www.spectorstorybox.com

www.ingramcontent.com/pod-product-compliance
Lightning Source LLC
Chambersburg PA
CBHW020621120726
47905CB00003B/886